The PRINCE and the PORKER

PETER BENTLY   DAVID ROBERTS

ANDERSEN PRESS

PIGNATIUS was passing the palace one day
when he saw ten fresh buns left to cool on a tray.
"Mmm," thought Pignatius. "I'm sure that it's fine
if I just try one bun. That still leaves them nine."

"Delicious!" he said as he chomped on that bun.
And the next – and the next – until soon there were none.

"I wonder," he thought, "if they've made any more?"

"I think I'll just check." And he crept through the door...

Pignatius was eyeing a big jar of cream
when the cook scurried in and let out a huge scream.
"He's eaten the prince's fresh buns, **every one!**"
"**Whoops,**" thought Pignatius. "I think I'd best **run!**"

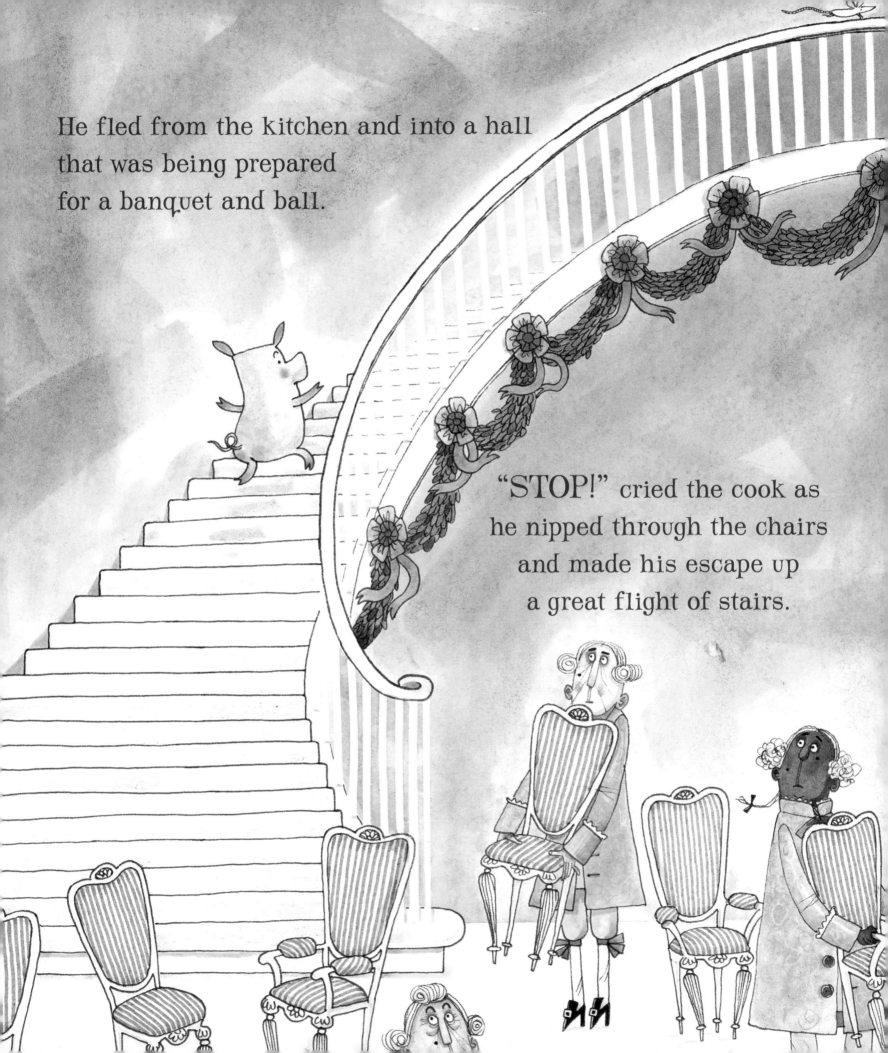

He fled from the kitchen and into a hall
that was being prepared
for a banquet and ball.

"STOP!" cried the cook as
he nipped through the chairs
and made his escape up
a great flight of stairs.

"I wonder who sleeps in this chamber?" he said,
as he entered a room with a four-poster bed.
The bedroom was splendid.
The pig was impressed.
He chuckled, "There's even a dressing-up chest!"

He had to agree that he cut a fine dash
with his buckles and breeches
and blue satin sash.
"What larks!" he exclaimed as he added a wig
that hid half his face (it was slightly too big).

He admired his reflection
from front, back and side.
But what was that noise
on the landing outside?

Then the cook and the butler, six maids and a groom,
plus several footmen burst into the room!
Pignatius grinned nervously back at the crowd,
but to his astonishment...

... everyone **bowed!**

The butler said, "Pardon this dreadful intrusion!
Your Highness, I fear that there's been some confusion.
The cook is mistaken, it's quite clear to see.
Now, what does Your Highness desire for his tea?"

"Gosh!" thought Pignatius. "They think I'm the prince."
And he said, "For my tea, I'd like... chocolate and quince!"
"At once," bowed the butler. The pig thought, "What fun!"
And he cheekily added, "And bring a fresh bun!"

Then he ordered,
"A cinnamon tart,
nice and hot,
and two jelly trifles –
the biggest you've got!
Three tubs of syllabub,
four treacle rolls,
five figgy puddings with
custard (six bowls).
Seven gateaux,
eight gooseberry pies,
nine fondant fancies
of extra-large size,
and lastly," the pig said,
"I almost forgot –
ten gallons of cream!"

And he gobbled the lot.

Then it was time to inspect the new guard
who were neatly lined up by the gate in the yard.

"Now for more fun!" thought the mischievous hog
and he ordered the soldiers to hop like a frog.
He made them do cartwheels and gallop and leap,
till they all ended up in a big tangled heap.

Then he blew the head gardener's pumpkin to bits!

And startled two duchesses out of their wits.

"Now," said Pignatius. "I fancy more grub.
Bring me some sweets in a very large tub."
Pignatius was munching a mouthful of mints
when into the hall strode...

... the genuine **prince!**

Then the butler took hold of Pignatius's wig,
pulled it and gasped, "Goodness gracious...

... A PIG!"

The cook cried,
"I knew that I wasn't mistaken!
I'll have him for sausages,
gammon and bacon!"

She turned to the
prince as he stood
in the hall
and told how Pignatius had
hoodwinked them all.

"Do you seriously mean," said the prince with great glee,
"that you truly believed that
this porker was ME?"

"Pig," he declared, "you've
been nothing but trouble.
However, I might have
some use for a double!"

Pignatius now gets to eat chocolate and quince
and he sleeps in a chamber next door to the prince.

But once every week,
he has had to agree
that he'll dress as the prince
and go down to have tea
with that terrible dragon...

... the prince's Aunt Alice,
when she comes every Thursday
to visit the palace!